HEARTSTRINGS

A START THE MUSIC ROCK STAR ROMANCE

BOOK THREE

EMMA JAY

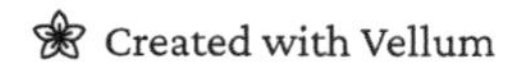
Created with Vellum

CHAPTER ONE

Sawyer

I HATE BAND MEETINGS. I mean, we are in the biggest band in the country. We have people to take care of literally every need we have. Why do we still have to go to band meetings?

And then Ava Darcy sits next to me. She smells amazing, and expensive. I want to lean in and breathe her in, and I might have, if we'd been alone. We've been dancing around each other for weeks.

She's our new media coordinator—and our manager Max's daughter. Yeah, we were all pretty surprised when he told us he had a college-age daughter because we didn't think he was that much older than us. She's graduated now, and joined our tour a few months ago as our media consultant, and has been driving me out of my mind ever since.

As I try not to stare at her, I look at her hands, long manicured nails that I can instantly see trailing down my body, now opening and closing on a computer tablet.

"Ava has some exciting news for us," Max announces.

I shift in the plush chair in the meeting room in the studio we've built, wondering what fresh hell she has for us. The band has gone through way too many changes the past year, and I'm not really wild about them.

First Hugh hooked up with a girl, and Jase with her best friend, and they're both married now. Then Oliver looked up an old girlfriend—okay, she wasn't just an old girlfriend, but you know. So they're married now.

Then my partner-in-crime, Callan, hooked up with the lead singer from our opening band, and now they're married.

So they're all wanting to slow down the touring and spend more time in the studio, citing The Beatles, but man, I love being on the road. I love the freedom of it.

Beside me, Ava draws a deep breath, bringing me back to the issue at hand.

"We're going to have a documentary crew follow us on tour."

"We're doing what now?" I demand.

"It's a huge opportunity to expose you to people who might not know who you are, or who know who you are but want to know you better. We will have a documentary crew following us for six weeks as we tour Europe."

I heard the "we" in there, but she hadn't said she was going to come with us to Europe. I have a lot of questions, but none I want to ask in front of everyone.

"I don't know," Hugh says, his mouth turned down in a doubtful expression. "How much access are we allowing them? I don't know if I want a film crew following me around."

"Well, obviously they'll be at rehearsals and sound checks and concerts. Probably a few afterparties. They do want more personal things, like interviews and some interactions with you and your wife, for example, but this isn't going to be a gotcha piece. It's not an exposé. It's in our favor."

Hugh and Jase exchange a glance that says they don't buy that. I'm not sure I do, either. I look at Max, but he's beaming with pride at his daughter.

"Did you ask for this?" I ask Max.

"I've been fielding requests for a while, and I've turned them down again and again, but Ava convinced me now is the time, to capitalize on your current visibility."

"Ava did." I turn my gaze to her, but she doesn't look at me.

"They'll join us in London next week, and will be with us until Portugal. I'm really excited about this—it can showcase you as a group, your international fandom, and also you guys being tourists. I know you've toured Europe before," she adds quickly. "But it's still something different for you."

"And we don't get a say in this?" Oliver asked. "I am not sure I want Suzanna filmed and showcased. She's still in school."

"We can make concessions for that," Ava said. "I don't want her made vulnerable either."

She doesn't sound like a twenty-two-year-old. She sounds like a woman who knows exactly what she wants.

I swallow that thought back. Yes, she does know exactly what she wants. I know that firsthand.

And it might get me killed.

Ava

Sawyer corners me near the sound booth after the meeting. My heart, which was still pounding from presenting my news, kicks into a higher gear when I drop my gaze to his lips. Then I look over his shoulder to make sure we are alone. I don't know who's still in the meeting room, where everyone else has gone.

Despite that, I cannot resist resting my hand against his chest, and I feel his heart is beating like crazy, too.

"What are you doing?" he asks, his voice low, and when I start to drop my hand away, he cups it over his chest. "You're going to get us caught."

"We won't get caught. I made sure I'll be the only one to see the raw footage."

"You don't think your dad is going to want to see it?"

"Oh, sure, but I can easily distract him."

Sawyer narrows his pretty blue eyes, fringed with lashes so dark, it looks like he's wearing eyeliner. "Do you *want* to get us caught?"

I shake my head instantly, though I have to admit the danger is part of the turn-on. A very small part, though, because Sawyer is sexy as hell.

And I'll be honest, a younger version of me would want to get caught, to get my dad's attention. I don't need that anymore. I'm here to show him how mature and successful I am, despite him.

"We won't get caught." I don't know why I say that with such conviction.

"You like living on the edge."

"You're right here with me." I'm fully aware that he has more to lose than I do. After all, he's been part of my dad's life longer than I have been.

But I don't want to think about that now. I want to think about how I'm all alone in this room with the sexiest man I've ever known, and he's looking at me like he wants to devour me. I am completely on board with that.

He's held himself back, and I know it's been a challenge for him, because I've seen coverage on his social life—never the same woman twice. I'm actually pretty impressed he hasn't gone out with anyone since we started...whatever this is. He's not sleeping with me—yet. I have to admit, the anticipation is pretty damn sexy, too.

I tilt my chin up and he lowers his mouth to mine with a groan. His lips are soft, his kiss starting out sweet until I touch my tongue to his lower lip. Then he pushes me back against the wall, his hands on either side of my head, and parts my lips, tangling his tongue with mine, hungry for me. I wind my arms around his shoulders and slide my fingers into his hair, making sure he doesn't move away unless I want him to.

God, kissing him is delicious. Matching the rhythm of his kiss, savoring all the heat, breathing him in, the smell of leather from his wristband, the musky, masculine scent of him. I want to smell him on my hands the rest of the day. I've actually toyed with the idea of a leather wristband, though I'd never wear it—not my style—just so I can smell it when he's not around.

Yes, I'm twenty-two, not twelve, but I may be a little obsessed. I won't say in love. Not yet. I do have some restraint. I think.

Very little.

He's better at it, and it takes me a minute to realize he has me pinned between his arms so he won't be tempted to touch me. I lean forward, pressing my breasts against him, but my jacket is so tight I can't really savor the feeling.

Then he breaks the kiss, his gaze focused on my mouth. He gives a little curse as he pushes away from the wall, then looks out the narrow window in the door to make sure the coast is clear. He must see someone, because he edges away from the window and looks back at me, lifts a hand toward my head.

"You look..kissed."

I feel my cheeks warm, and my lips spread in a smile. "You were there."

He rolls his eyes. "I can't help with your lips, but maybe you should fix your hair."

I reach up and feel the strands that have come loose from my twist. I loosen it completely, sweep it all together with my hands and attempt to twist it back into its sleek style, using his expression as a mirror. He shakes his head, pats the top of my head. I can feel the bump of hair there. I blow out a breath, loosen it and start over.

"Here."

He moves forward, finger combs my hair down, then back, holding it in place until I can get the clip around it. Then he slides his fingers down the sides of my face and nods, drops his hands away and steps back.

Once my appearance meets his approval, he pivots and slips out of the studio.

SAWYER

LONDON, baby.

Yeah, we've been before—a couple of times—but it is one of my favorite cities. I love the pubs, the history—both political and musical, the way it tries to squeeze modern places in between historical places. I love the people, the clubs, all of it.

I stop myself from thinking what it would be like to show Ava around. Has she been? I don't know, but I can guarantee she's never been to the places I want to take her.

I. Need. To. Stop. Thinking. About. Her. I should just go out, get laid, forget about her altogether.

But no other woman appeals to me.

We have two days in the city before the documentary crew arrives. Good. I get checked in to our hotel in Mayfair, and immediately head for the doors.

"Where are you going?" Oliver asked, his tone affronted.

"Soho, man."

"I thought we were all going together tonight."

Right. We always go see local bands together, as a group. That's how we'd found Elizabeth's Folly, the group that opened for us in the States, and now is soaring in their own right.

"Let me know when you head down, and we can meet up." I'm too wound up to go to my hotel room. I want to get out of here while I still have freedom to move without having to think of anyone else. I love my band, but we spend a lot of time together, including the plane ride over, and it would be nice to be on my own for just a couple of hours. Not think about anyone but me.

I almost collide with Ava walking in the door, because she's looking at her phone, not where she's going. The phone falls, and I swoop to catch it before it hits the ground. When I straighten to hand it to her, her eyes are wide.

"Thank you. That would have been bad."

Before I can chide her into paying attention to the world around her—we're in London, for Chrissake—she notices I'm heading out.

"Where are you going?"

I spread my arms as I step out onto the sidewalk, turning back to face her. "London, baby!"

She smiles, turns and says something to the doorman, hands over her big purse, scooping a smaller purse out of it, and charges after me.

"Let's go!"

I stare. Hadn't I just said I wanted to be alone? But I'm not going to send her away. Why? None of your business why. Instead, I look down at her heels. She's always wearing heels, and those snug little suits.

"Those aren't the most practical way to see London."

She waves a hand. "I'll be fine. I wear heels all the time."

Yeah, I know, but, "I'm not going to be carrying you if you twist your ankle." Most of the streets are paved, but there are some uneven places.

She lifts an eyebrow, something I've always wanted to be able to do. "I'm not going to ask you to."

But by the time we get down to Soho, her steps are lagging. I steer her into a shop with more practical shoes, and point at the displays.

"Pick something. I'll buy."

She looks from the flat shoes to me. "I can't wear shoes that flat. My feet are like Barbie's."

I look at her askance.

"You know, the doll? Her feet are permanently formed for heels."

"Your feet are hurting. Put on some practical shoes."

With a sigh, she moves closer to the wall to inspect, selects a pair of white ones I still wouldn't call practical, but I see the relief on her face when she sinks down into the soft insoles. I nod, take the bag with her heels, take her hand, and were out the door again.

I don't see much of the sights after that. I'm watching her take it all in, head craned back, occasionally releasing my hand to spin around and look, take some pictures with her phone, only to grab my hand again and let me lead her.

We're miles away from anyone we know, and I could kiss her any time I want, not care about who sees, but that would be selfish. I want her to see the sights, and I want to enjoy watching her. Holding her hand is enough.

Jesus, who the fuck am I?

She pulls me into a shop with definite bohemian vibes, something I never would have associated with Ava, who's always, always, dressed in suits, her hair either pinned up severely or down and straight as an arrow. I realize that other than knowing we have fantastic chemistry, I know next to nothing about her.

She moves between tables and shelves with less efficiency than I'm used to seeing from her, and she lets go of my hand to load up on trinkets.

"For you?" I ask, inspecting her selection of wild jewelry, bracelets and such, when she approaches the cash register.

She looks over at me. "No, my best friend. She would go crazy in this store."

"Your best friend is...that." I gesture to the pile of bright and clunky pieces. "And you're...this." I swing my hand up and down the length of her.

She smiles at the clerk and completes her transaction. "Variety is the spice of life."

"Is she, like your college roommate or something?"

She looks sideways at me. "She was my best friend in high school, and yes, we went to Northwestern together, but we lived in a house, not a dorm, thank you very much. Like, literally, thank you very much, because we couldn't have afforded it if you hadn't made my dad so much money."

I laugh. "Happy to help in the education of the next generation."

She rolls her eyes. "I'm not that much younger than you."

"Ten years," I say. "And I've had much much more life experience."

"That's why I'm here," she says, tucking her arm through mine so the side of her breast brushes my bicep. "Life experience."

I grunt. Is she talking about me giving her life experience, or the tour? I'm not sure I want to know.

I think she might want to go into some other stores, but she doesn't seem to care to shop too much. She's happy to linger in front of a window and move on. I'm happy to let her, because then I can look at our reflection in the glass and see what other people see.

The rock star and the princess. I'm dressed in slouchy jeans, a t-shirt from a video game, and a faded ball cap pulled low, so it kind of pushes my hair out to the sides, and shades. Yes, I'm trying not to be recognized, and it's worked so far, hasn't it?

And next to me is this goddess, not quite as tall as me now that she's out of those heels, hair and makeup perfect, expensive suit—and shoes, though I can't see them in the reflection—and this smile of delight on her face that warms me through.

Goddamn, I love seeing her smile.

Again I think about kissing her, but I hold back. I don't need to make this about sex. I want to make it about her joy.

We pass through Soho and into Covent Garden as it starts to get dark. She turns to me.

"You know what I really want to see is the London Eye."

"Well, I mean, you can see it," I tease.

"You know, what I mean. I want to ride on it."

I frown. For one thing, it's not all that close to where we are. For another, "I understand it's hard to get tickets."

She leans close to me. "You're Sawyer Fucking Powell. I bet you can get us tickets."

What did I tell you? Princess. What else did I tell you? I love to make her smile.

So I hail a ride to take us to the Eye.

As expected, the line is long, because people love to see the city at night. As expected, there are signs advising to book in advance. But look, like she said, I'm Sawyer Fucking Powell. I have thrown my weight around before to get what I want. And I want to see Ava smile.

So I take her hand and walk to the front of the line.

CHAPTER TWO

Ava

I REALLY DIDN'T EXPECT him to charge up to the front of the line, dragging me behind him. And I'm a little amused when he lifts the ribbon directing the line, ignoring the curses and shouts from the other tourists, and heads straight for the tour guide at the front of the line. She steps back, surprised.

"Sir, the line?'

"I'm Sawyer Powell. We want to buy two tickets."

"Sir, everyone else behind you already has their tickets—they bought them online? I advise you to do the same. Come back tomorrow. We're sold out for the night."

"For the night?"

"Yes, sir."

"Do you know who I am?" He whips off his hat and sunglasses, and the girl takes another step back, shaking her head.

"No, sir."

He's flummoxed by that, and I try not to laugh. I give his hand a little tug. "Sawyer, it's okay. We don't have to—"

He turns toward the line, pulling out his wallet. "I'll buy someone's ticket." He holds the wallet over his head, then opens it and looks inside. "Shit, just American money, but it's three hundred dollars. Three hundred dollars for two tickets."

I'm vaguely aware of the crowd shifting, some looking away, some grumbling, some consulting each other, but mostly I focus on him. His expression is sincere, the cynicism from earlier gone as he holds up the American bills.

Finally a man edges his way through the crowd, holding up two tickets, and he and Sawyer make the exchange. Before the man—a heavy-set, balding American, based on his Old Navy t-shirt—heads out of line, he wants a selfie with Sawyer, who obliges, then turns back to the tour guide, tickets in hand.

She looks past him to the rest of the crowd, who are restless and irritated, but she decides not to make any more of an issue as she motions us into one of the capsules.

I guess I didn't realize each capsule could fit so many people. I kind of thought we would be on our own, but that's fine. Maybe it's best we're not. He leads me over to the window —the only time he's let go of my hand was when he made the exchange—and puts me between him and the window, bracing his hands on the bar on either side of me as the capsule lifts.

He doesn't say anything, but I feel his breathing against my ear, feel his chest move against my back. It's a little erratic, so I turn my head to look, and see he's gone pale as we rise over the Thames.

"Are you okay?"

"Not really a big fan of heights."

"Oh my God." I turn completely in his arms then, still braced between them. "Why are we here, then?"

"You wanted to do it, I didn't know if you'd get another chance. Turn around. You're missing it."

I am aware I'm missing it, but I don't want him miserable, either. "Sawyer."

"Turn around, Ava. I'll be all right. Look. It's beautiful."

The warmth in his voice has me turning, and wow, yes, it is beautiful. The sun is setting over the city and the lights below are flickering on below us.

It's breathtaking.

Sawyer's arms tense on either side of me, the higher we go, and I try not to wonder what it means, that he'd make this sacrifice for me, just because I said I wanted to do it. I get the idea he thinks I'm something of a princess, since I grew up with money, but Max didn't really have a very big part in my life until the last few years, so while I had money, I don't think you could say I'm actually spoiled.

I mean, did he think I was going to throw a fit if I didn't get my way? Have I ever? I hate that this question has niggled its way into my brain, when I thought he was just being nice.

I could ask him, but he seems miserable enough.

Now that he's unmasked himself, more people are noticing him—well, everyone noticed him because he made such a scene —but I see people taking surreptitious pictures, before a few more brave souls approach and ask for selfies. He indulges them, probably because he'd inconvenienced so many by making that scene, and I'm left to enjoy the view on my own. But at least now he's not focused on being afraid of heights.

I smile to myself. I never thought Sawyer was afraid of anything. He always struck me as the boldest of the group, so it's interesting to see his weakness firsthand.

"Miss, would you like a selfie?"

His voice against my ear sends a shiver of longing down my spine, and I hand over my phone—should be safer than using his phone—and we turn with our backs to the window and he lifts the phone to take a couple of shots. All I see is the lit-up structure of the Eye behind us—and the way he's looking at me.

Oh. My. God. My panties damn near melt right off.

If anyone sees this picture, they will be able to draw some conclusions.

Maybe he's right. Maybe it was stupid of me to bring this documentary crew on now.

So maybe, if we want to avoid detection, tonight is the night to act.

Just when I'm about to suggest that to him, my phone starts to ring in his hand, and my dad's picture looks down on us from my phone.

Sawyer nearly drops it, and this time I'm the one to catch it, and swipe to ignore the call before I turn back to him.

"Probably wondering where we are." Though I'm not sure anyone knows we're together. I mean, out together. Exploring together. Not *together* together.

He grunts. "My phone's been buzzing pretty much this whole time. Probably wanting to know the same thing."

"Do we care?" I ask.

"You might want to let your dad know where you are."

"Do I let him know who I'm with?" I know the answer already. I just want to see his face, which is horrified, as expected.

I turn my camera toward myself, take a selfie that makes it clear where I am, and send it to Max as way of explanation.

"Should we join them, once we're done here?" I ask, stepping just a little closer to him. My heart is thundering, both at his nearness and my boldness. I know he's attracted to me. I know he's torn about it. And I know I shouldn't be teasing him. But I can't help myself.

"I...should," he says with a croak. "Was my idea."

"Hm." I turn back to look out the window. In the reflection of the glass, I see Sawyer watching me, not the view, and I don't bother to stop the thrill that runs through me when I see the longing in his eyes.

When we complete our rotation and step out, he guides me with a hand at the small of my back.

"I'll take you back to the hotel, if you want, then I'll go meet them."

I make a noncommittal noise. If I have my way, he won't be leaving the hotel any time soon.

He hails a cab, which I will say I'm grateful for. I'm in pretty good shape, but this has been a long day. He pulls out his phone once we're inside and starts texting, staying silent. I ignore him, looking out at the city at night.

I may be quiet, but my mind is working. How am I going to get him out of the cab and upstairs? Because once we're upstairs, I have no doubt I can get him to stay.

Am I living dangerously? Absolutely I am. But it's going to be so worth it.

The hotel is closer than I thought, and I have to scramble for a reason to get him inside.

If he was looking at me, I wouldn't need a reason, just a couple of undone buttons, or a hike of my skirt and I'm sure I could convince him, but he's looking at everything but me.

"I think I'll go get a drink at the bar before I head upstairs," I say, as lightly as I can manage.

"Why don't you come out with us, then?"

I shake my head. "I don't want to be around everyone, and have to worry about getting back. Just a glass of wine before I head up, to relax me."

He mutters something, types something, then settles up with the cab driver before sliding out of the cab to follow me inside.

I hope he doesn't see my triumphant smile in the reflection of the door.

SAWYER

I LOOK DOWN into Ava's lovely blue eyes and stroke my thumb down her cheek. We're in the hallway outside my room, and I'm not sure just how she got me here. No, I'm not drunk. I'm just under her spell.

"This is such a bad idea."

She gives me a pout that has doomed men from the dawn of time. "Is it?"

She knows it is. I'm the lead guitar player in the biggest band in America, not known for my ability to hold down a relationship. For even wanting to hold down a relationship. She's my manager's daughter, ten years younger than me.

Nothing about this is smart. But I cannot resist her.

Not any longer.

She parts her lips under mine and I dip my tongue inside, just a tease, but am I teasing her, or myself, I'm not sure. I want to pin her to the wall behind her, press into her, and I think she'd probably not mind, but she's...different. Everything about her is different. Different from me, different from the other girls I've known.

It's ridiculous, the way I'm shaking.

She gives a little sigh into my mouth and winds her arms around my shoulders, bringing her firm breasts against my chest, and I'm instantly hard. I have...had fantasies about those breasts. It takes all my willpower not to cup one in my hand right now.

But I can't resist running my hand up and down her back,

knowing how it will affect her. Feels weird, though, because she's wearing this little pink suit, and I've never kissed a woman in a suit, or even a woman who might wear one.

I'm telling you, Ava is different.

I lift my head to look down at her. She pressed back against the wall, her breath coming fast, her gaze focused on my mouth.

"Let's go inside, Sawyer."

My head swims. There is nothing I want more. But I've been friends with her dad a long time, and the two of them are trying to build a relationship. If I take her to bed, what will that do to their relationship?

If I was a stable guy. If I was closer to her age, or she was closer to mine.

So many reasons to say no. I dig deep for the word, and back away.

Disappointment turns the corners of her eyes down. "I'm not a virgin."

I don't know how that's supposed to make me feel, but I'm pretty sure jealous was not her intent. Hell, that surge even surprises me. I'm not even sure what to call it at first, but the idea of another man's hands on her makes me hot, and not in a fun way.

I know, ridiculous, considering I have no idea how many women I've been with, and I started when I was much younger than she is.

"I know what to do," she says, oblivious to my thoughts. "I know how to please you."

I wanted to teach her how to please me, but I push that thought aside. "Ava. That has nothing to do with this, and you know it."

"Do I?" She reaches between us and unbuttons the top two buttons of her suit jacket.

I am painfully hard when she exposes the swell of her breasts over what looks like a lacy bra. No blouse under the suit. I can't tear my eyes away.

Suddenly the door behind her is open and she backs inside. I don't know how, or when, she got my key card, but I stumble after her, cursing my own weakness.

I reach for her and she steps back, lifting a hand to free her hair from its sleek, pinned up style. Her straight chestnut hair falls to her shoulders and, hell, she looks so young. I stagger back, reaching for the door and the last of my sanity.

If she was just some twenty-two-year-old, no big deal. But my friend's daughter—man, this is some kind of fucked up.

But I stare, and as I do, she unbuttons her jacket the rest of the way. The breasts she reveals are exquisite, encased in lace that leaves little to the imagination, and I cannot wait to get my mouth on them. Aware she has my undivided attention, she unhooks her skirt and shimmies out of it to reveal matching panties—the smallest fucking panties I've ever seen.

I'm rooted to the spot when she steps toward me, her movements sinuous, at odds with her usual all-business stride. She lifts her mouth in offering, and I take it.

We've been stealing kisses for weeks, and let me tell you, that is really hot. I'm not accustomed to feeling guilty about sex, so I wonder if the guilt makes it hotter, or if the secrecy, or if we just have this amazing chemistry.

I prefer the latter.

I savor her mouth, tracing her plump lips with the tip of my tongue, diving a little deeper and tasting the tartness of the wine she'd had in the bar. I always think it's funny she orders wine while the rest of us are drinking hard stuff. I think she tried to order some fruity drink once and we ragged on her mercilessly, so now she sticks with wine.

She wants to appear so sophisticated. Who she's trying to impress, I'm not sure, because I'm already impressed as hell.

I slip my hands beneath the straps of her bra as we kiss, ease them down as I smooth my palms down her upper arms. I'm tormenting myself, going slow because she's Ava, and I want to give her every chance to change her mind.

She slides her hands up under the hem of my t-shirt, over my abs, up over my pecs, her fingers threading through the hair of my chest. She doesn't try to remove my shirt—I think she doesn't want to break the kiss—but her fingers stroke over skin I long ago stopped thinking of as erogenous, and I want to explode.

I open my eyes to look at us in the mirror, and see the reflection of her back, her hair swinging down to the clasp of her bra, her ass high and tight in the thong underwear.

I can't help myself. I slide my hands down over her ass, watching the contrast of my dark hands against her pale skin. She parts her legs just a bit, and I have to close my eyes again, to renew my fight for the control she seems determined that I lose.

She slides her hands around my back, and her manicured nails scrape my skin.

Okay, that's it. I take a step back and strip my shirt over my head, then wrap an arm around her waist and drag her against me. Goddamn, she feels good against me, skin to skin, looks so sexy with her hair loose, her bra straps looped over her arms.

I unhook her bra and watch as the cups fall forward, carrying the garment to the ground. Christ, she's perfect, her breasts full and round, the nipples not quite hard, but they will be when I get my mouth on them. Her shoulders are a little tense, and I drag my gaze away from her tits to meet her eyes.

"We can stop whenever you want," I say, but my voice is rough with everything I'm holding back.

She reaches for me, strokes her fingers through my hair. "I'm not changing my mind."

Thank fuck.

I pull her close, cupping her tits in my hand, her nipples hard now against my chest. I kiss her mouth, glide my open mouth down her throat, wincing as my stubble reddens her tender skin. Then I lift her breast to take her nipple into my mouth, sucking on it, feeling her entire body surrender as she arches her back and pushes her tit deeper into my mouth. I tongue her nipple, rolling it around, then turn my attention to the other.

I release that one wetly, then look up at her and draw her back toward the bed.

I sit, parting my legs for her to stand in between, sliding my hands down over her ass to her upper thighs, bringing her closer.

I can smell her arousal. It fills my senses, and I pull her even closer so that she has to part her legs over my hips to kneel on the bed, her sweet pussy hovering over my crotch.

I slip my hand down to push aside her thong and find her drenched, so fucking wet. I watch her face while I glide my fingers over her folds, dipping inside her, circling her swollen little clit. The lines in her throat are tight, her eyes closed, her head back so her hair is brushing the arm I have around her, holding her to me.

I lift my hand to my lips and lick her juices off my fingers, then push them back into her, fucking her with shallow little thrusts, just knuckle-deep. I add a third finger, and she makes this sweet little mewling sound, and drops her chin so she can meet my eyes.

"I want you to fuck me, Sawyer."

"I plan to."

"Then stop screwing around and get naked."

She breaks her grip on my shoulders and dismounts, stepping out of her thong, naked in front of me, that pretty pussy completely bare, so inviting. I lick my lips.

She poses, turning out one leg so I can see her pretty pink folds, but she is just out of reach.

I know what she wants, and if I was a stronger man, I'd deny her because that's just what kind of guy I am. Instead, I strip off my t-shirt, unfasten my jeans, kick off my boots and lean back, letting her look her fill, too. Her eyes are a little wide, and that amuses me. Then she swallows and turns toward the dresser. In the reflection I see her paw through her little purse, and then she turns back with a couple of packets of condoms, which she tosses on the mattress beside me.

"I hope they fit," she says, and walks back over to me, not quite as confident as before. "I hope I fit."

I have the condom on and I'm ready by the time she returns to my reach.

"Oh, you'll fit. Come here, Beautiful."

CHAPTER
THREE

Ava

Do you know what it's like to want something for ages, and to finally get it? It's terrifying, that's what it is. But here I am, naked with Sawyer, his enormous cock aimed right at me, so here we go.

I part my legs over his thighs, taking his dick in my hand, hearing his intake of breath, and I guide him to my entrance. I'm wet, but he's so thick, my body has trouble adjusting. I push my hips forward, deciding not to be delicate about it, and he groans.

"Fuck, you're so tight. Jesus, Ava."

His words send a flood of wetness to my pussy, and I take in another inch. Then another. I feel spread wide open by the time I take him all in, by the time my ass touches his thighs, his pubic hair tickling my clit. He's watching me, his eyes heavy-lidded, and I slide my hands down over his chest, down to where we're joined, then up again as my muscles adjust to him.

And then I begin to move, holding onto his shoulders,

sliding up and then taking him deep again, deeper than before. I look down and watch myself fuck him, watch him slide in and out of me, and wow, is it erotic. He grasps my ass in both hands and guides me the way he likes, the angle, the pace, and I meet it, wanting to please him, my own desire flaring damn near out of control as his cock drags along my inner walls, as my swollen clit brushes his groin.

My clit demands more contact, but I'm savoring the feel of him filling me, the sensation I've craved for so long. I circle my hips on his, and he groans again, lifting into me, and I gasp, tossing my head back.

He leans forward and captures my nipple in his mouth, and I feel his teeth. My clit pulses, my pussy contracts, and he does it again, scraping lightly before soothing it with his tongue, then moving to my other breast.

"Your tits are gorgeous," he says against the wet nipple, his breath and stubble combining to arouse me more. "Good goddamn thing you hide them because I would be hard every waking minute."

The idea that I could arouse him like that gives me a wicked idea. Maybe I need some form-fitting blouses. Pretty bras. Lots of peek-a-boo lace.

"I love the idea of driving you crazy."

"You do. Those tight skirts, those gorgeous legs, that ass."

He drags his fingertips up the cleft to the small of my back, and I gasp as my nerves seem to explode out from the contact like the finale at a fireworks display.

"I think about fucking you. I think about eating your pussy. Now that I've seen it, I will think about that all the time."

"Are you going to eat me later?" I ask, breathless, as I loop my arm around his shoulders and ride him in shallow thrusts.

"Oh, you know I am."

He tightens his arm around my waist, and before I know

what he's doing, he has me on my back on the mattress, my legs spread wide, my cunt missing him filling me. He pushes my legs up, opening me, kneeling on the mattress and lowering over me to swipe the flat of his tongue over my pussy.

"So sweet," he says, then taps his tongue against my clit until I go completely tense,, then he circles his tongue at my entrance.

I'm mindless. I can't hold him, so I grip the comforter beneath me, spread my legs wider, and only one word fills my head.

"Please!"

"You want to come, sweet Ava? You want to come on my tongue, or on my dick?"

My gaze flies to his, and I...can't decide. "Fuck me," I say, and he smiles, kneels over me and slides in deep. I arch my head back into the pillow as he pushes into me, slides out, then back again, slowly. And that's the rhythm he sets, slowly out, slowly back in, so I can feel all of him against all of me, each time. I don't know why I thought he was going to pound me—maybe he had been thinking about it but this...this is so much better.

His head is bent as he watches his cock slide in and out of me. I look, too, for a minute, because it's so hot, but I love watching him. He lifts his head, tossing his hair out of his face, and increases the tempo.

"Tell me if this is too much," he says, his voice rough. "I don't want to hurt you."

My heart does a little trip at that. "It feels so good."

"Yeah? You like that?" He increases the tempo, and I part my legs wider. "You feel amazing, Ava. God, I'm going to feel you around me every time I look at you."

My heart did another stutter. "I'm going to feel you inside me every time I look at you. Every time I touch myself."

His jaw tightens, and he picks up the pace, not quite pounding into me, but close.

"Show me how you touch yourself, pretty Ava."

Holding his gaze, I bring my fingertips to my lips, lick them —though I know I don't need to, I'm so wet—and slide my hand down my body, between my breasts, between us to slide over my clit.

My nails brush against the base of his cock, but he doesn't seem to mind as I circle my clit, much the same as he did, then slide my touch up over it.

"I feel it," he mutters.

"Do you want me to come?" I ask, breathless, teasing my clit lightly with my fingertips.

"No. I'm going to make you come. I just want to know what to picture when I jack off."

He looks down to see my fingers, then I lift them to his lips. He sucks them into his mouth, running his tongue over them, then drawing on them in a way that I can feel in my pussy, and I pull my fingers free to stroke over my breasts.

"Goddamn, Ava, you are so fucking sexy."

And then he pulls out of me.

I groan my frustration as he slides down my body, holding my legs open and lifting my hips to his mouth in the smoothest move, and then he's licking me, his tongue teasing my entrance, then flicking up to my clit, stopping as I wind up, ready to explode, then again, before covering my cunt with his mouth like he's deep-kissing me, only it's my cunt and my clit and...

The sound that bursts from me when I come, pumping my hips against his face, doesn't sound human, sounds wild and guttural. I keep moving against him, terrified he'll stop before this sensation curling through my blood ends, but he lifts his head anyway, and this time the sound I make is one of frustration before he eases back over my body, guides his cock to me and slides in.

The colors that had been fading burst again and I open to him, meeting his thrusts, riding out this new layer of my orgasm before he catches his breath, slams deep into me, and I feel the pulse of his own orgasm deep inside.

Both of us are breathing heavy when he cups my head in his hand, kisses me wetly, tasting of my own juices, then drops onto the bed beside me. I turn onto my side, not able to get enough of him, sliding my hands over his chest, his throat, down his arm over his tattooed band circling his bicep before resting on his hip next to his flagging erection.

He turns his head on the pillow to look at me. "You want to go again already?"

I smile. "I feel like it's going to be awhile before I get enough." I've wanted him for so long, we've been teasing each other for so long. The orgasm he gave me is only now fading.

He rubs his fingertips up and down my arm. His smile is tender, fond. I've never been in love before, and I'm pretty sure what I'm feeling now isn't love, but I also feel like I'm well on my way.

This could be bad. This could be very, very bad.

I SNEAK out of his room before dawn, figuring I won't encounter anyone I know in the hallway at that time. They would either have already come back to the hotel earlier, and they wouldn't be up and about yet. This is one of those times where it's a good thing we have rooms on the same floor, and a bad thing.

Still, I breathe a sigh of relief when I get into my room and close the door behind me. I cross the room to dig my charger out of my still-packed-and-in-the-center-of-the-room bag and plug in my dead phone. I never let my battery die, but I guess I'd had too many apps open or something that drained my battery.

Immediately my screen fills with missed calls and messages from Max. I send him a quick reassuring text that I'm not dead in the Thames, and go take my shower. I'd slept a little in Sawyer's room, but it wasn't very restful, so I climb into bed, setting the alarm to go off an hour later than usual—don't want to raise suspicions that I was out all night—and turn out the light.

My alarm isn't what wakes me in the morning, though. It's my father, banging on the hotel room door. I check my still-charging phone for the time. Seven thirty. I've been asleep maybe two hours.

I pad to the door and open it enough to peer through the crack.

"What is it?"

"The documentary crew is here. They arrived last night. Why didn't you answer your phone?"

I hadn't even read the texts or listened to the voicemails. I feel my face heat. "My battery died. I'm sorry."

He raises his eyebrows. "You never let your battery die."

"No, I know. Jet-lag, I guess." Way to think on my feet after barely any sleep. I toss my still-damp braid back over my shoulders. "They're here? Did they say why they're early?"

"They said they want to get some B-roll footage of the guys exploring the city.

"They understand these are rock stars, right, not likely to be getting up this early." I narrow my eyes at Max. "Why are you up this early?"

His face reddens a bit. "Just needed to get stuff done."

"Uh-huh." His messages had been coming through all night, so I wonder when he got any sleep. "What do you need me to do?"

"I need you to introduce the band to the crew, let the band know what the expectations are for today, and guide them around." His turn to narrow his eyes. "Where were you last night? I thought you were going to meet us at the club."

"I was but then I decided I wanted to ride the Eye, and after that I was ready to turn in early."

"You look like you didn't get any sleep."

"Strange room. Lots of noise."

He studies me a moment. I don't know what he is thinking. I just don't know him that well.

"Can I count on you for this?"

"Yes, of course. It's my project, I've got this."

He stands there a moment longer.

"Yes?" I ask.

"Are you going now?"

"Are they waiting now?" It's so early.

"Just to be available to them, so I can go get some sleep. I gave the producer your number."

I hadn't thought we would have to babysit the crew every moment, but maybe it did make sense to be available for them the first day. I nod, which seems to satisfy him, and he finally turns away, leaving me to close my door, turn to face my bed longingly before I go get dressed.

CHAPTER FOUR

Sawyer

I DON'T KNOW what I expect my interaction with Ava to be like the following day, but I guess I didn't expect her to look at me like butter wouldn't melt in her mouth. I know she's not mad at me, so she must be putting on a show so she doesn't let on what went on between us last night.

Today's suit is a pale blue that shouldn't turn me on, but I know now what it's hiding, those gorgeous tits, that bare pussy. And that mouth she's holding so primly was wrapped around my dick only a few hours ago.

Fuck, I cannot sit in this meeting with a hard-on, but whatever she thinks she's doing by acting so cool is having the exact opposite effect.

She wants to introduce us to the production crew. Great. We have four people to add to the entourage. I look down the table to see a woman about my age, maybe younger, pretty in a no-nonsense way, and three dudes, all younger, and two of them are looking hungrily at Ava, who is not paying any attention to them.

She's looking at the band, kind of like a teacher who wants to tell us what to do.

Yeah, that's pretty hot.

"So today, the crew is just going to follow you around the city as you do your sightseeing," she tells us. "You can go together, you can break off into a couple of groups, but they do want to see you interacting with each other."

"The viewers want to know about your relationships with each other," the woman, who Ava introduced as Claudia, spoke up. "We want to see the casual stuff, the things you talk about, the names you call each other."

"You do not want to know the names we call each other," Jase says with a grin.

"You know what I mean," Claudia says. "We want to see the real you."

"Going to be tough, with a camera following us around," Callan says.

"You'll get used to it," Claudia promises. "Pretty soon you'll forget we're here."

"Pretty soon? How long are you with us?"

"Until Portugal," Claudia says.

Weeks and weeks away. I roll my shoulders to get rid of the unease.

"Going on the plane with us and everything?" Oliver asks.

"That invitation was extended to us," Claudia says, but her tone is...odd. Like she's not sure.

"So why can't you just watch us interact then?" Oliver asks. "I'd like to go with my family today, not with these guys."

Claudia and Ava exchange a glance. I wonder what they'd been talking about that led to that look.

"That's fine," Claudia says. "I can get something with you and the others in Paris."

Oliver's jaw is set firmly. "I want to take my family around there, too."

"That's fine," Ava says this time. "Perhaps you can schedule it so you spend some time with the band, some time with your family."

He grumbles. "We should have been consulted before you arranged this."

I get it, he wants to protect his family. And I'm not crazy about the documentary idea either. I don't really see what the benefit of having this documentary is, but I also don't want to piss on Ava's parade. I mean, we're sleeping together now. That doesn't mean I'm her boyfriend, but I feel like I should support her, you know? So I jump to Ava's defense.

"She's trying to help us out, not make our lives miserable," I say. "It's not going to be a twenty-four-seven thing, right?" I ask Claudia.

"No, you'll still have your privacy for the most part. We won't record on the plane, for example. And we will leave Suzanna out of this, as discussed." She addresses the last to Oliver.

"Thank you."

"We do want to interview you, together and separately, starting tomorrow," she said. "We all know your history, so we kind of want to get a sense of where you are today. What makes you who you are now. I don't want to do any gotcha questions, so I want you to think about that before our interviews tomorrow. They'll be before and after soundcheck."

I kind of resent being told what I'm going to do by this stranger, and as I look around the table, I think the other guys are feeling the same. But I've determined to support Ava, so I smile at Claudia, nod, and rise.

"Let's get started, then."

I catch Ava's gaze and see a small smile of thanks—at least, that's how I interpret it—as we file out.

I guess I kind of imagine it as something you'd see in a Beatles movie or something, us moving about in a pile, swinging from lampposts, that sort of thing. But Claudia makes it clear she wants us to act "normal," interact like we usually do, which isn't easy with two cameras following your every move. She keeps telling us we'll forget she's there, but we don't. Finally she gives up, saying she'll try again in Paris.

"Thank you for stepping in like that," Ava murmurs, falling into step beside me as we head back to the hotel.

I glance over at her, and man, she looks so tired. Desire and guilt war within me. She's tired because I kept her up all night. "No problem."

"Are you guys going anywhere tonight?"

I press my lips together. "Asking for you, or for Claudia?"

"What? No, I'm just curious."

I can't resist giving her just a little bump, but she's caught off guard and stumbles in her heels, so I catch her forearm. Once I make sure she's steady, I brush the side of my hand against the back of hers. She looks up at me, her cheeks tinted a pretty pink, before she steps away.

When we get back to the hotel, everyone goes their separate ways. The other guys are glad to get back to their ladies—except Callan, whose lady is on her own tour, so she hasn't joined us here. I kind of expect he'll want to do something with me, though he hasn't said so.

But no, once we get into the elevator, he heads off to his own room without a word. Max, too. Everyone's kind of in their own world. Weird.

Look, we're in London. Sure, I've done the sightseeing thing, but I'm not planning on sitting in my hotel room tonight.

So I text Ava.

Ava

THE TWO OF us head out to a club in Soho to see a local band. I've seen him play, many times, and I love watching him lose himself in the music, love watching his fingers move on the strings.

I haven't seen him play, however, since he used those same dexterous fingers on me. I can't wait.

But now I'm enjoying watching him watch this band. They're good, I guess. They're not as good as Elizabeth's Folly, or Ranger Danger, the band opening for Obscure Magic now.

So, yeah, Sawyer had texted me when I was at dinner with Claudia, asking me if I wanted to come out with him to see the band. I had hesitated, because I didn't want to tell Claudia where I was going, but then my dad showed up and joined us, and it was surprisingly easy to escape after that.

At first I wasn't really sure what Sawyer wanted, and I might have been a little surprised that he really did want to go see a band.

I'm wiped out, but I'm not going to tell him that. After all, as he said, we're in London, and why would we sit around in a hotel room when we could be out seeing the sights?

It's nice, just the two of us. When the band goes as a group, they're easily recognizable. While Sawyer was recognized, all it meant was that we were escorted to a VIP section, which keeps us apart from people who want autographs and selfies with him.

We're on our second drinks, and his hand is on my thigh

under the table. Just there, not moving, not caressing, just resting. Kind of...possessive. I like it.

Look, I know Sawyer. I mean, I know who he is. He's not a happily-ever-after guy. I have no expectations of that, and even if he wanted that, I'm twenty-two. I'm not ready to settle down. So I'm...well, I don't know what I'm doing. I'll figure it out at some point, right?

I haven't had a boyfriend before. I've been busy with school and interning at the local TV station. Sure, I've dated, I've had sex, but there's never been a guy in my life week after week.

Seems kind of dangerous that Sawyer is my first. I have next to no experience, and he has all the experience.

Though I don't know if he's had a real girlfriend before, either.

I shift in the booth, crooking my leg on the seat, so his touch moves to the inside of my thigh, and he glances over at me to see if that's okay with me.

Um. Yes.

After a few minutes, though, I notice he's...playing guitar chords? Like, his fingers are pressing the chords on my inner thigh.

"Are you...playing their music?" I lean forward to ask.

He shifts his hand to the top of my knee and rests there. "Um, yeah."

"You can just do that? Figure out their music like that?"

"Um. Yeah." He looks over at me. "I've been playing a long time, Ava."

"Yeah, but you can hear a song one time and figure it out?"

He motions toward the band. "It's not really complicated music. And I'd probably have to hear it again before I could play it, but yeah, I can figure it out."

"That's—wow, that's a skill."

"I mean, I hear the music, my hand makes the chord. Not all the time, but yeah."

He seems flustered. I have never seen him flustered. He's cool, confident, savvy, and I like that about him. But this is fun, too.

I wrap my arms around his arm, the one that's been on my leg, and snuggle into him. "Play some more."

He looks into my eyes for a minute, his gaze questioning, then he turns back to the band. "Not sure I can perform under pressure."

I shift my head so my hair falls against his bare arm, and I watch the strands catch in the hair of his arm. "I bet you can."

He grunts, and a few minutes pass before he relaxes enough to get into the music again. I release his arm and scoot away, feeling bad now for taking him out of his enjoyment of the music. But he grabs my leg and pulls me back over, turning to look into my eyes as his fingers press chords into my skin. I hold on to him, afraid of losing my balance even on this seat, and look back at him while his callused fingers caress my thigh.

It is the hottest thing I've ever experienced in public, and I part my thighs a bit. He doesn't take the bait, instead, sliding out of the booth and holding out a hand to me. I take it, not sure where he wants me, but knowing I'm willing to go.

He tugs me toward the exit, and into our waiting car, then onto his lap.

I panic for a minute, before his lips claim mine. The driver, Dave, works for the band, and we're trying to keep this a secret. What if he tells my dad?

But I push the concern out of my head as Sawyer slides both hands up my thighs, under the hem of my skirt, stopping just before he gets to where I want him the most. My hair falls forward to frame us, and I lift my breasts in my hands, needing the touch.

His mouth beneath mine is mobile and hot, and I know exactly what I want him to do with that mouth. I wish we were completely anonymous, that he could go down on me right here and no one would ever know, ever see us again. But I have to face Dave tomorrow, and I could never, if he knew we'd done that.

Thankfully, we get to the hotel pretty quickly. I take a moment to smooth my hair and my suit before I slide out of the car, not meeting Dave's gaze as he holds the door for us. Sawyer rests his hand on the small of my back as we enter the lobby. I chance a look around, hoping I don't see anyone I know.

Fortunately, we make it to the elevator without being recognized, and though we're alone, Sawyer doesn't make a move, just holds my hand and watches the numbers light up over the doors. He lets go of my hand when the doors slide open, and we walk as casually as we can manage down to his room. I wonder briefly why his room and not mine, but I guess it's more expected to hear sex sounds from his room.

But once we're inside, he sweeps me into his arms, circling me around toward the bed, where he drops me, shoves up my skirt and yanks off my panties, tossing them in a wad over his shoulder. He looks down at my pussy for a minute before he parts my legs wider, pushing one finger, then two, into me, stroking slowly, watching my face as he does. I arch into him, at the same time scrambling to unbutton my jacket, letting it fall open to reveal my pretty lacy bra.

He gives me an appreciative grin, then removes his touch.

"On your knees."

I scramble up because yes. Maybe I should be more graceful or whatever, but I need him inside me, and me being on my knees means he can touch me all over. I shed my jacket but leave the bra on, and he positions me so that we can see ourselves in the mirror of the dresser.

As I watch, he doesn't even undress, just unbuttons his jeans, rolls on a condom and slams into my pussy.

The sound that comes out of my mouth doesn't even sound human, and suddenly, he's leaning over me.

"Are you okay? Did I hurt you?"

I mean, yeah, it kind of hurt, but it was pleasure with pain, you know? So I shake my head and he does it again.

He's so deep. I didn't know it was possible to be so deep. I gasp, and grind back on him, and he thrusts forward again. I'm kind of swimming in the sensation of how he feels inside me, and how we look in the mirror. I can see him thrusting against me, his hands on my hips holding me steady. God, it's hot, especially since he's completely dressed.

"You're so wet, baby. So wet. Were you this wet in the club?"

"In the car. Thinking about Dave seeing us."

"Jesus, baby." He goes still, deep inside me. "You want someone to watch?"

"I don't know if I want it, for real, but the idea of it turns me on."

He leans over and kisses my shoulder. "Dirty girl," he laughs in my ear, and rises again to fuck me, his movements faster, more deliberate, each stroke hitting just right. He sweeps his thumbs up over my butt cheeks, parting them just a bit, and very lightly strokes my butthole.

I clamp down on him, the orgasm sweeping through me with a force I never expected, that I didn't think I could get without touching my clit. My cunt floods with wetness, and his movements are faster, slicker, deeper.

I lift one hand off the mattress and shove it between my legs, circling, flicking my swollen clit. He sits back on his heels and pulls me over him, still fucking but I'm on top, kind of, and he reaches around to push my hand out of the way and takes over the caress.

My eyes pop open to look at us in the mirror, my legs spread over his, his hand between them, me pumping and bouncing, and then...I'm pure feeling, pure pleasure, like it's shooting out of every pore as I come, as I ride him and feel him come, too.

I drop bonelessly to the bed as he heads to the bathroom to take care of the condom, then returns to the bed naked and wraps me in his arms for a long, sweet kiss.

"You're the most fascinating woman I've ever met," he murmurs, before turning me in his arms to spoon me, and we both fall asleep.

CHAPTER FIVE

Sawyer

I FORGOT Claudia wanted to talk to the band after soundcheck, and she wanted to talk to us as a group. I get that she wants to see us interact, but we...not all of us are the same when it comes to being in front of the camera, right? Like Callan will stay silent if he can get away with it. Hugh will be self-deprecating, Jase will make wisecracks. Oliver will be the smooth one, and I'll be the charm.

Okay, maybe I get why she wants to interview us that way.

But even as she sets us up in the chairs, gets her camera guys and sound guy set, I'm looking past her for Ava.

She'd slipped out of bed after I'd fallen asleep. I get it, because she doesn't want anyone to know, but I'd missed her.

Yeah, I know. Me, who never sleeps with a woman more than one night in a row, who never sleeps over. I'd reached across the bed and been disappointed when I didn't find her.

Look, you might think I just want to fuck her, and I mean. She's gorgeous. So yeah, I do. But I like talking to her, like listening to her. Right now I just want to look at her, see her smile at me while I sit through this interview.

She doesn't smile, though. Keeping it cool, I know. Still, I like looking at her.

So much, that I miss Claudia's question, and when I snap my attention to her, I see a knowing look in her eyes.

Ah, hell, the last thing I want is some documentarian trying to catch us in a "gotcha" move. I need to talk to Ava and remind her to be careful with Claudia. Honestly, I'm not sure who has more to lose if Max finds out.

Ava

I'M NOT sure I'm hiding my feelings very well as I watch Sawyer take the stage. One of the things I lo—I admire about him is his confidence. He has that loose-limbed gait, and he loops his guitar over his head, and it rests against his hip. He bends his head as he plays, and God, watching his fingers dance over the fret, remembering how he'd pressed them against my thigh.

Guh.

"Ava."

My dad's voice beside me makes me jump a foot, move back from the edge of the stage to turn to face him.

"Yeah, what's up?"

"I haven't seen much of you this trip."

I press my lips together, because we are still, you know, working on things. "I've been busy with the documentary crew."

He makes a noncommittal noise and folds his arms over his chest as he looks at the band. "Are you having fun?"

"Sure. Who wouldn't have fun touring Europe with a band

like Obscure Magic? I'm glad we planned to spend a few days in each city, though. Good for the documentary."

He makes that noise again. "Not sure how good of an idea it is, if I'm being honest. Not sure I should have let you talk me into it."

I turn to him. "You were excited about the idea."

"Sure, because who has documentaries made of them? Big bands. But the idea I had for this and the idea Claudia has are different. I thought she'd do more history of the band, you know, but she wants their interaction and I feel like that's more intrusive than we planned."

"I mean, yes, I wish they were more on board, but I feel like this is the best theme to get them new fans. I mean, you know how they are together, and I just feel like that's going to charm people into listening to them, you know? They might relax more as they get used to the cameras being around. Just give it time."

He still appears doubtful but doesn't press. And honestly, I don't know what else to talk to him about. I feel awkward watching Sawyer while he's here. Plus, conversation isn't the easiest when there's a concert going on a few feet away, so we just stand in awkward silence, my arms wrapped a little tighter around myself.

Sawyer grins over at me, and his grin fades when he sees Max next to me.

God, I hope Max doesn't notice. But when I chance a glance over, he seems lost in his own little world. I wonder what he's thinking. But like I said, conversation is hard. So we just settle in to watch, side by side.

I stiffen a little when the band comes off the stage before their encore, because Sawyer heads right for me. But he just gives me a strained smile, then walks by. Max pats him on the back. I do my best not to follow him with my eyes, but I see him grab a bottle of water and drink it down without stopping, crunch up the bottle into a little ball and toss it into the recycle bin. Maybe he senses me looking because he turns and grins. I think—I hope—Max's attention is elsewhere.

Sawyer switches out guitars, fiddles with this one for a few minutes, while the noise of the crowd grows more and more adamant outside. It makes me tense as the band lingers, laughing and talking.

Finally they stroll back out, past me and Max. He does not seem worried in the least that they take their time. I realize then that Claudia's crew had been recording the band, and they hadn't acted weird or self-conscious like they had during our tour of London. Maybe they were still on their concert high. Maybe they were getting used to the crew along.

I relaxed marginally.

Then it was time to go out after the concert.

Sawyer

Ava is a little uptight when we all meet up in the bar of the hotel after the concert. We do this after every concert, though the crowd starts out bigger and thins out earlier every time, now that most of the guys are attached. And everyone came on this trip—wives, girlfriends, stepdaughter. Claudia and her crew are here, without cameras, that I know of. Look, I'd just like them to get their job done and move on, you know? Leave us to do the rest of the tour in peace. I just don't have a lot of trust in them.

Ava is sitting with Claudia and trying hard not to look at me. I know this because I'm trying hard not to look at her. She's back to her buttoned-up self, the tight hairdo, the suit and heels. I know it turns me on because I know what, and who, lies beneath. One day I'm going to ask her what compels her to dress this way. Does she think she'll be taken more seriously? I mean, she looks gorgeous, but she would be just as beautiful if she dressed more casually, like Callan's girlfriend Delaney or —

I don't know. I'm not trying to change her. I'm just curious, is all.

And while I'm thinking all this, I miss whatever question Callan just asked me. He's looking at me expectantly.

"Huh?" I ask.

"Where's your head?"

Is that what he'd asked me? I feel my face heat. I'm definitely not going to answer that question. He'd already suspected something between me and Ava back in the States. Maybe he's just looking for confirmation of his suspicion. I need to be more careful not to give him that.

"Sorry, man, just tired, I guess. Jetlag?" I push my glass away, give him a few moments to repeat his question if he's going to, then I stand. "Going to head up early, I guess."

Like, the first one to go up. Even Oliver and Lindy are still here. Now everyone is giving me a look like Callan. I mutter the same excuse I gave Callan, and despite my best effort, I meet Ava's eyes before I turn toward the door and back into the lobby. I'm not sure how to get her to my room again tonight.

I hear footsteps behind me soon after, and it's Chelsea, Jase's wife. I have to hide my disappointment, and at the same time hide that I'm hiding my disappointment. I smile, which I hope she doesn't see is forced.

"Calling it a night?" I ask, resuming my path to the elevators and press the button.

She gives me a look. I don't know her well enough to be able to read it. We step into the elevator along with a few people coming in from a late night. Some of them recognize me so I do the autograph/selfie thing and they get out of the elevator happy, leaving Chelsea and me.

"We didn't sleep great," she offers finally. "The people in the room next door were having some wild sex. Like a lot. I would have thought this hotel would have more soundproofing, but there you go." She gives me another unreadable look. "Don't be surprised to get some payback."

The door slides open to our floor, and she precedes me.

"And you might want to be careful when she leaves your room. That could really cause some trouble."

She walks to her room—right next to mine—bids me good night, and goes inside.

Great. So she knows. Or suspects. I don't know if she's told Jase. Callan also suspects. I wonder if I can get away from the documentary crew long enough to talk to them, to beg them to keep quiet.

Because walking away from Ava right now just...isn't going to happen.

I CAN'T STOP myself from watching Ava as we drive through Paris in the bus. She'd dressed more relaxed today, for travel, in jeans and a button-up shirt, her hair in a looser style. I know I shouldn't be noticing, because there's Max and there's the camera crew, and Chelsea and Jase giving me a look—that answers my question about whether or not Chelsea discussed what she knew with Jase—and Callan giving me a look. Maybe I'm starting to get paranoid, but I can't help it.

Ava's pressed against the window like a little kid, straining to see everything. She'd told me last night that this was the stop she was looking forward to the most, and I wish we had a day like we'd had in London before the documentary crew arrived.

And yes, last night she came to my room, and I let her in despite the warning from Chelsea. Maybe I'm stupid, maybe I'm foolish, maybe I'm reckless, but I'm not ready to give her up.

I can't risk sitting beside her because I won't be able to stop myself from touching her, so I content myself with watching her.

We pull up to the hotel, close enough to the Eiffel Tower to take your breath away, seriously, and I'm not really that big into landmarks. But watching Ava's reaction makes me smile.

"What's going on?" Oliver asks, frowning at me.

"What do you mean?" I brace my hands on the backs of the bus seats and raise up to swing my feet, like I used to do when I was a kid on a field trip.

"What are you smiling about?"

"What do you mean? We're in Paris." I'm watching Ava through the bus windows, watch her enter the hotel, and want to hurry in after her.

I don't need to go to the desk to get my key, but I see Ava there, leaning over the desk to talk to the woman, her eyes bright, excited words pouring out of her lips.

Excited French words. I hang back a little, marveling, hoping no one notices I'm waiting for her. We walk together to the elevators.

"I didn't know you spoke French."

She gives me a look, her eyes bright. "I had a very good education. But I'm glad I'm not getting here until now."

"At the ripe old age of twenty-two."

She sticks her tongue out at me. "Old enough to appreciate the culture and the history."

"Is that what you're doing today?" I glance down at her shoes, low wedges. "Looks like you're dressed for walking today."

"Ah, I should probably go with you and the documentary crew," she says as I hold the door open for her.

Oliver, Lindy and Suzanna are in the car with us, and Max and Callan.

"Nah, we'll be fine. You go do what you want to do," I tell her, then, hell. I'm not her boss. Her dad is. I look at him, and lift my eyebrows in hopes he'll second my encouragement.

"Will you be okay by yourself?" Max asks her.

"I can go with you," Suzanna pipes up.

A realization hits me then, that Ava and Suzanna, at about sixteen, are closer in age than Ava and I are. Whoa. That is...not a great feeling. We haven't had a lot of clashes over that, like, she doesn't seem that much younger, but maybe that's because she acts older than she is, and I'm a big kid. Still, the age thing hasn't hit me until this minute.

Lindy and Oliver confer while I'm having my revelation, and Lindy reluctantly gives permission as long as they're back by dark, and both have their phones. They all exchange numbers.

We reach our floor. Well, what I thought was our floor. Ava and Max step off, but Max holds his hand out, stopping the rest of us.

"Everyone wanted a view of the Eiffel Tower, so we had to get rooms on two floors," Max explained. "This is our floor. You're two floors up."

My gaze instantly snaps to Ava's. Won't be so easy, her getting to my room now. She gives me a tiny shrug and turns back with her dad.

"We'll meet in the lobby with Claudia and the crew in an hour," Max tells us, and the door slides closed.

I rest my head against the back wall and hope that Lindy and Oliver attribute it to my frustration with the documentary crew. I would love to be seeing Paris with Ava. Maybe some day I could bring her back, but it's not the same as watching her see it for the first time, you know?

Whoa. Someday I could bring her back? Where is my mind?

Oliver says something to me when I exit the elevator ahead

of them, but I don't process it, just kind of wave in acknowledgement and head to my room.

The curtains are drawn back and I have a stunning view of the Eiffel Tower. I snap a picture and send it to Ava before I can think about it. Then I wait for her response.

A few minutes later I get a picture back of Max standing by the window looking out at the Eiffel Tower. My stomach lurches.

Are you staying with Max? I text.

I stare at my phone for several minutes waiting for her response, but of course, if he's there with her, she isn't going to respond right away.

Finally her response pops up.

Of course not. That would be weird.

It *would* be weird, and the relief that washes through me is even weirder. I don't know how to express that via text, so I just say, *Have fun and be careful.*

She sends me a selfie of herself sticking her tongue out at me. I laugh, but again I remember how young she is. I don't feel that much older than her, but I've had ten years' more experience. If she and I end up together, what will she miss out on by settling down so young?

Why does my brain keep going in that direction? It's been only a few days, and I've never even thought about settling down before. Yet with Ava....

Another text pops on my screen, this time from Max, and my stomach clenches.

Let's get going.

CHAPTER
SIX

Ava

"WAS it everything you thought it would be?" Sawyer asks, his fingers playing in my hair as I lay in the crook of his arm, looking out his window at the Eiffel Tower.

It's our last night in Paris. Tomorrow we head to Berlin. We won't be there as long, which is fine with me. My German is terrible.

I twist my head to look up at him. "Paris? Or this?" I motion between us.

It's funny to me how quickly I've gotten used to spending the night with him. I love being in his arms, love listening to the beat of his heart, the rumble of his voice in his chest. I've never felt so at ease with a lover, never felt so much like myself. Maybe it's because I've known him for a while.

"I meant Paris, but if you want to throw a compliment or two my way, I'll take it." He shifts onto his side, lowering himself on the bed so we're nose to nose.

"I could stay here another week, easy. Maybe even a month."

"And do what?"

"See everything. Eat in cafés every day. Walk along the Seine every evening." I link my fingers through his and bring our joined hands up to rest on his chest.

"Maybe you can stay," he says. "Meet us later in the tour."

I'm surprised how his words hurt. "I have a job to do."

"We could get along without you for a few days."

"Do you want to get along without me?" I know this has been stressful for him, hiding what we have from my dad, his friend. Maybe he'd like a break.

He pulls his hand free of mine and wraps his arms around me, pulling me against him.

"I can't imagine getting along without you," he murmurs. "I just want you to be happy."

My heart, in my chest, does a weird tumble that I've never felt before. My pulse picks up, my whole body is warm as I look into his eyes. It's not arousal. It's not affection.

It's...more. And it's intoxicating.

"Maybe I'll come back once the tour is done," I posit. "Instead of going home."

His eyes grow a little somber. "That might be good."

I know their schedule. I know they have a few big stops on their way back to California. So he couldn't stay with me.

Does he want to?

No, of course he doesn't. Sawyer Powell is not a man who gets attached. Like famously doesn't get attached. He'll just break my heart down the road.

Why can't I make myself care?

. . .

Sneaking into my room is a little challenging, being as we're on a different floor, but better me encountering my father in the hallway instead of Sawyer meeting him there. I'd slept in a bit, too, so the sun is already up. Risky and reckless. It would be one thing if the truth would just hurt one of us, but I'm afraid it would hurt Sawyer more than me.

I jolt when a door opens and Claudia steps out into the hall. She's wearing a man's shirt and her hair is a mess, and she jumps about a foot when she sees me.

We size each other up. I know she's seeing the same guilt on my face that I see on hers, though I don't understand why *she* would feel guilty. I'm in my same clothes from last night. My hair is down and wonky from sleeping spooned up with Sawyer.

"I'm just—I heard the elevator and I thought it was room service. I thought I'd meet them out here." She glanced over her shoulder, back into the room.

The temptation to try to see who is in her bed is strong, but I resist. "Sorry to disappoint."

"Yes, well. I didn't think anyone else would be out this early."

"No? Ah, well, it's not that early." I try to smile but I have no idea what it must look like.

She gives me a knowing look. "Early enough."

I do not want to linger out here. What if my dad comes out? One thing to have another woman know I was with someone all night—she doesn't know who—and another to have my dad see me. He would have questions. I walk past her toward my room.

"I'd better get a shower before we head out," I say. "I'll see you later."

I fumble with my key card—not the cool image I want to

present to her—and escape into my room, breathing a sigh of relief.

Sawyer

It's getting harder and harder to keep my distance from Ava, to pretend that we're not spending every night together, that I'm not falling for her.

She rides in the front of the bus with the documentary crew, doesn't even look at me. She's stronger than I am. But she has more to lose, I guess. We're lying to her dad. Okay, not lying outright, but not being honest, and we both know it's going to upset him when he finds out.

If he finds out, I mean. If.

Berlin is a shorter visit, just three days, and we don't have the documentary crew following us around while we're sight-seeing, so we all kind of go off and do our own things the first day. We need the distance, I think, even though it's just been a few weeks. And I'll be honest, I'm tired of the judgey looks I'm getting from the guys. Not all of them. I don't think Oliver knows—he and Lindy and Suzanna are kind of insular—but Callan, Jase and Chelsea do, and Maya is Chelsea's best friend, so probably Maya and Hugh do, too.

Honestly, I don't want to go sightseeing so I just head to a pub. Yeah, I have to sign a few autographs and do a few selfies, but I find a quiet table and order a drink.

And then Callan walks in. He looks around for a minute, spots me, goes to the bar too, orders a drink, and heads over to me.

"What are you doing here?" I ask when he slides into the wooden booth.

"What are you doing here?" he echoes.

"Just wanted some alone time."

"You're not hiding from Ava, are you?"

"No." I lift my beer to my lips. "Why would I do that?"

"I don't know, man? Why would you?"

I blow out a breath and sit back, my shoulders against the hard back of the booth. We've known each other for too long to play games. "Just say what you want to say."

"Your secret is going to come out. And when it does, it's going to be seismic."

"What are you talking about?" I'm not patient enough for his vagueness.

"Too many people know. This many people cannot keep a secret. And if things start going south with the two of you, Max is going to notice, too, and figure it out."

"Things aren't going south, why would you think that? We just figure if we spend too much time together, Max will for sure notice, and we're avoiding that."

"Man, I think you need to talk to him. Better you're honest with him than he finds out on his own."

I study my beer for a moment. "After Assago, when we're on our way home."

Something shifts in Callan's eyes. "I thought you'd tell me to fuck off, because it would be over by then."

I open my mouth, then close it. "I don't know, man. I mean, she's a lot younger than me."

"She is," Callan agrees slowly.

"She might not want to be in a relationship. She has a lot of living to do to catch up."

"Wait a minute." Callan leans closer. "Are you falling for her?"

I lift both hands from the table, kind of helplessly.

Callan's shaking his head. "It's just sex."

"No, it's not." Sure, there's a lot of sex, but that doesn't explain the lift I get when I see her, the warmth in my chest when I hear her voice, the excitement I feel when I'm waiting for her. How much I love sleeping with her in my arms.

"What does she think?"

"Ah." I can't look at my friend right now. "We haven't talked about it. Just taking it a step at a time. And I can't tell Max without talking to her first. Who knows what that would do to their relationship?"

"Something you probably should have thought about before you started sleeping with her," he points out.

"Goddamnit, was I this much of a dick when you started screwing around with Delaney?"

His face reddens, temper flashing in his eyes. "Don't talk about her like that," he says through his teeth.

"See how disrespectful it is?" I demand. "Just mind your own goddamn business."

His jaw is tight, and my stomach tenses, too. Callan says nothing, just drains his beer, slams the glass on the table and storms out.

Not only am I in danger of alienating Max, but my friends as well. And I'm not even sure how Ava feels.

SHE DOESN'T COME to my room that night. I'm restless, pacing the room, when she finally texts me well after midnight.

Can't. Complications, is all she says.

Well, what the hell? I think about getting dressed and going downstairs, but I don't really want to see anyone when my mind is one big tumble, wondering what she's doing, so I try to go to sleep, but I'm not really tired, and I miss having Ava beside me.

I don't see her until the following afternoon at sound check.

I'm tired and hurt, and none of that is helped when she avoids me. Shit. I mean, I know the doc crew is here, but I need to talk to her. All last night I turned over what Callan had said and I think he's probably right. I think we need to get this in the open.

But every time I approach her, she moves away. My frustration is making me incautious, and I finally trap her near the steps back by the bathrooms. I see she's wary, the way she looks over my shoulder, the set of her shoulders. I try to reassure her with a smile, forcing my own body to relax, even as I block her escape.

"Everything okay?" I ask.

"I just—couldn't get away," she says, not meeting my eyes.

"Max?" I ask. "I would have let you in no matter what the time."

She looks at me then, and her expression is pained. "There's just...stuff you don't know."

"Then tell me." I touch her arm. I sense she wants to pull away, and that hurts, but not as much as her feeling she can't tell me what kept her away last night.

She shakes her head.

"Callan thinks we should talk to your dad. Or just I can, if you want."

Her brows snap together. "What? You'd want to do that? Why?"

I can't help myself. I stroke the backs of my fingers down her pretty cheek. "Can we go somewhere and talk about it?"

She turns into my touch for the briefest of seconds, then pulls away. "Not now," she says, and hurries away.

I let her go, and she doesn't come to my room that night, either. She doesn't even text.

Honestly, I'm surprised to see her at the concert the following night. She's avoided me all day, and I guess I made it easy for her because I stayed in my room most of the day. I try not to imagine what she's doing or who she's with. I pick my phone up every two minutes, either wanting to text her or hoping she's texted me.

Nothing.

Another night of being restless. This time I get dressed and head out of the hotel.

CHAPTER
SEVEN

Ava

I DON'T KNOW why Claudia is suddenly so friendly. I mean, she's nice enough, but she doesn't give me a lot of space. She says she doesn't get to hang around with women her own age much—I mean, I don't know how old she is, but I guess we're the same generation. And like I said, she's nice. We go sightseeing and shopping and to dinner. I wonder if she shouldn't be working on the documentary, or if she's avoiding someone.

Maybe the man who'd been in her bed the other morning had been one of her crew and now she's regretting it. I haven't asked, because it's none of my business. Besides, I don't want her to ask me where I was coming from that night.

I miss Sawyer. I know, it's weird. But I haven't so much as passed him in the hallway, or seen him from a distance. I almost feel like Claudia is keeping me away from him on purpose, but she can't be, right? She doesn't know about us.

He's not texting me either. I mean, I never told him I changed his contact information in my phone so it won't say

SAWYER in big letters. I changed it to the first thing I could think of—Chandler, like from the show *Friends*, where he and Monica are hiding their relationship from everyone. Only they aren't just fooling around. They're falling in love.

Am I? I've never been in love before. I've never felt *this* way before, like being away from him is a physical pain, like all I need to make my day better is a smile from him, a touch. But I'm too young to fall in love, right? I've only just graduated college. I've never been out on my own. He's been living his dream for ten years and I haven't even really settled on what my dream is. I like what I'm doing now, but I don't know if this is what I want to do forever.

How do I know what man I want to be with forever?

No, it's way too soon to know.

But what else can it be, when my heart does this crazy triplet when I see him before the concert? As if he knows I'm watching him, he turns and meets my gaze, gives me the smallest of smiles, glances toward Max, then returns his attention to the rest of the band.

I promise, I'm not a jealous person. I'm not a princess, even though I know people think I am. But I haven't seen him in what feels like forever. I know he's busy, but I just want the smallest minute of his time.

I catch his gaze and motion for him to meet me back behind the stacks of touring cases.

He glances around, then widens his eyes at me. Is it weird I know just what he's saying? *Do you really want to risk it?*

I glance around for my father, but he's disappeared. I check, too, for the cameras. They are with Claudia near the stage. I think we're in the clear. I move out of sight, and hope he follows me. Still, when he does, I jump a little. Maybe I'm more nervous about this chance than I thought.

"What's going on?" he asks, taking my arm and drawing me farther into the shadows.

I look up at him and just...take him in. I feel like I have this goofy smile on my face while I'm looking at him. I have to shake myself out of it. We only have a minute.

"I just wanted to let you know that I'm not blowing you off. I just haven't really had time to myself lately, so I haven't been able to, you know."

A small smile curves his lips, and he brushes his knuckles down my cheek. "You know you could have let me know other ways, right?" He pulls his phone out of his pocket and swipes the screen, then taps his contacts. "I changed your name, so no one would know."

I straighten, wondering why I hadn't thought he'd have the same solution I did. "What did you change it to?"

"Monica. Like in *Friends*, where they—"

He doesn't get to finish. The feeling I've been struggling to name, that I've been doubting for days, makes itself known, and all caution flies out the window. I grip the front of his t-shirt and pull him toward me. I see his smile just before I claim his mouth, sinking into him, this man I love.

"What in the hell?" Max's voice carries over the noise of the backstage, and for a moment, there's silence, except for the opening band on the stage.

Sawyer draws back and closes his eyes, just a moment, in resignation, before he turns to face Max.

I look past Sawyer and read the fury on my father's face. Afraid he'll do something foolish, I edge around Sawyer to stand between the two men, my hands behind me, not to hold Sawyer back, but to show Max I'm ready to protect him.

Max looks from Sawyer to me, then jabs a finger at me. "I told you to stay away from him. Didn't I tell you to stay away from him? He's nothing but a fuck boy, and I should have known he would take advantage of you."

I feel Sawyer flinch, can't imagine how those words must hurt, coming from his friend as they did, no matter how mad Max is. My protective instincts—that I didn't know I had—rear up. I push my face toward my father's. "I don't need you to take care of me. I did once, but not anymore. You don't get to tell me what to do."

Okay, that sounded very teenager-y when I'm trying to prove to the man—to both men—that I'm mature. I guess I just wasn't prepared for him to hit that button.

Gently, Sawyer closes his hands on my waist and draws me back, not behind him, but beside him, and he holds me there, his hand not possessive but—reassuring. Temper runs through my whole body. I tremble with it.

"Cool it, Max. It's not like that."

His voice is calm and easy, though when I look up at his face, I see tension in the lines that fan from his eyes, in the set of his mouth.

"You have your hands on my daughter."

We're drawing a crowd now, and I glance past Max to see Paul, one of the cameramen, naturally. Why did I think a documentary was a good idea? I glance at Claudia, wanting to ask her to get Paul out of here, but she is watching Max, her hand curved over her mouth like she's worried about something.

"I'm in love with your daughter."

Sawyer's voice is low and somber, cutting through everything else. *Everything* else.

I whip my head around. Sawyer's not looking at Max now. He's looking at me. His eyes are softer, his expression one I've only seen when we were in his room.

"Are you—serious?" I manage, but I know the answer already. I can see it. I know him.

"I love you, Ava. I'm sorry it had to come out this way, but..." He trails off, his eyes crinkling at the corners, and he lifts my hand to his lips. "Yeah, that's why I've been kind of going nuts the past couple of nights."

I can't talk at first, the words catching on the lump in my throat. I don't often have lumps in my throat so it takes me a minute to figure out what to do. Also, it's hard to think when the man you love is looking at you like that.

"Sawyer. I—" I've never said these words to anyone, never even felt the urge to say them. "I love you, too."

He lets out a breath, then smiles and lifts a hand to push my hair back from my face.

My father grabs his hand, spins him around, and punches him in the mouth.

Sawyer

It hurts like hell singing through a split lip, and I bit the inside of my mouth when Max punched me, too, so the harmonies are a little off tonight. Every time I open my mouth, I wince.

But Ava loves me, so totally worth it.

This wasn't how I wanted everything to come out in the open. Not how I wanted Ava to find out, not how I wanted Max to find out. I didn't want the band to have to deal with the drama, especially right before a show.

They saw Max punch me, they didn't say they told me so, didn't say much of anything to me, to be honest. They're not even looking at me now. I can feel their—no, not resentment. Frustration. I need to make it right.

I glance toward the wings, where Max usually watches the show. He's not there. Ava's not, either. The camera crew is, naturally. Fuck those guys for being around to catch all the drama.

Okay, no, I can't blame them for everything going to shit, but they didn't make it easy for us, did they? I mean, not that we would have been skipping down the hall hand in hand without them there, but we might have figured things out sooner.

I need to talk to Max. I need to make him understand.

I need to talk to the band, to apologize for fucking everything up when they had definitely warned me this would happen.

But most of all, I want to talk to Ava. I want to revel in what we just discovered, and maybe...maybe...think about what's next.

Ava

I SIT across from my father at the pub, the wooden booth offering both protection from onlookers and privacy for us. His eyes are still hot, his nostrils flared, and I am not in the mood for it.

"I know you still think of me as a little girl," I say after the waitress brings me a glass of wine and him a pilsner. "But I'm not. There was a time you could have told me what to do. There were times I needed you and you weren't there. When there were storms, and school events and so many other things, and you weren't there—and I never even heard so much as an apology for why. So you can't come now that I'm an adult and tell me who I can and can't spend time with." I almost said "sleep with," but Sawyer's admission earlier has me modifying the thought.

Max's jaw hasn't relaxed since this whole thing went down. "I've known Sawyer a lot longer than you and I know what kind of person he is."

"You called him a fuck boy. I thought he was your friend. Why would you call him that, in front of everyone?"

He has the grace to look down. "I mean, he's got the reputation. He earned it."

"So what? That's not who he's been the past few months. And even so—"

Max leans forward, eyes boring into mine. "Months? This has been going on for months?"

I shift in my seat despite my determination to remain composed. "There's been interest for a while. It ratcheted up once we got here. And I made the first move."

He braces his hands against the edge of the table, like he's trying to stop himself from doing something.

"Jesus, Ava, that doesn't matter. He should have known to rebuff you."

I want to ask if he thinks I would have accepted that, but he really doesn't know me well enough. "He's a good man, Max. He cares for me." He loves me. But I haven't wrapped my head around that new information long enough to speak the words. "You know he's a good person. You've known him for years."

"I mean, hell, Ava, we've been through a lot together."

I could bring up that he'd spent that time with Sawyer and not with me. Instead I watch him, my jaw clenched just like his.

And I see the moment he realizes what he's said. Good, at least he's not oblivious. But he's also not finished.

"He's not a serious person. He has no sense of responsibility. He doesn't even have a house, just lives in a hotel, even though we're all trying to get him to invest his money while he can. He's got no interest in anything beyond today. He doesn't think of the future."

"So what? That makes him a bad person? It's not like he's as old as you are. He's in his early thirties. He's got time, he's got money. Let him live his life." I lean forward, my hands flat on the table. "I didn't come here so you would take care of me. I came here to spend time with you, so we could get to know each other."

Now he looks sheepish. "And I haven't been doing a very good job of that. I'm sorry."

"Neither have I." I square my shoulders and resist the urge to look away. "I guess maybe it takes more effort than either of us thought."

He reaches across for my hands, takes them both in his. I honestly cannot remember the last time he showed me affection. Like I said, he wasn't around when I was young. He's only been back in my life for a couple of years, and all that time, he's been really awkward with me.

So the sensation is weird.

He has strong hands, slender, but big. Young me would have been so comforted by them. But no sense dwelling on that.

"I will do my best not to interfere. And I want to make sure you and I, just us, get some time together over the course of the tour. Maybe...maybe then I won't be so worried that you'll get hurt."

My heart softens a bit as I admit to myself it's kind of nice he wants to protect me, late or not. "Fresh start," I say, as much to myself as to him. "And don't worry. I can take care of myself. But I need everything to be okay with you and Sawyer, Max. I need you to be, if not friends right now, at least not enemies. Can you promise me that?"

He tries to look tough, but a corner of his mouth hitches. "I can promise to try."

CHAPTER EIGHT

Sawyer

I DON'T GO into the dressing room after the concert. The band needs to talk without me. I know it maybe looks like I'm avoiding them, but not one of them looked at me while we walked off stage. They need to decide what they want to do.

But I'm not going anywhere. I'll face the consequences, and I'll make amends.

Ava and Max aren't back yet. That has me twisted up, too. Man, I hope I didn't fuck up their relationship. I feel like that needs to be fixed before she and I can go forward. I know, just by observing, that it hasn't been easy for them. I know it wouldn't have been easy for me.

So I sit backstage, on the stairs, fucking around on my phone until the battery gets too low. If my guitars weren't packed away, I'd noodle around, but...

The door to the dressing room opens, and the guys come out. Their ladies, who have been standing in a group far from me, straighten up, but an exchanged look is all it takes.

"Come on, ladies, we'll go back to the hotel," Maya says.

She, at least, casts me a sympathetic glance on her way out the door.

I slide off the touring case where I've been sitting, face the four of them.

"Am I out of the band?"

That takes Oliver aback. "What? No. Jesus, Sawyer. But damn, you might have screwed up our relationship with Max. All of us warned you about that."

I mean, Oliver hadn't, but I'm not going to argue.

"I'm not just sleeping with her," I argue. Had they not heard my declaration of love? Look, I've made one, ever, and it was in front of everyone. At least, that's what I'd thought."

"I'm not sure that matters to Max," Hugh said, his brown eyes mopey. "All he knows is that you are sleeping with her. And everyone knows your history with women."

Right, so I brought it on myself.

"This time is different," I insist.

"How do we know?" Jase asks.

"Isn't the fact that I say it is enough? Jesus, it's bad enough Max calls me a fuck boy, but you guys, too?" I rub the center of my chest, stung by the betrayal by these guys I've known over a decade, who I would say know me better than anyone. Maybe I earned my reputation, but they should take my word when I say what I have with Ava is more.

They should trust me.

I look from one to the other, and I don't see trust in their eyes. I don't know how to show them. Then I realize I don't need to show them. Ava's the only one who needs to know. She's the only one I need to prove myself to.

"If it comes down to it, and it's between Max and me, I'll quit the band," I say. "But I deserve the chance, like you all have gotten, to see if this is the real thing. I think it is. I'm just asking you for that."

Hugh had opened his mouth when I'd said I'd quit the band, but now they're all looking at each other.

"Please don't hurt Ava," Oliver says softly, and they walk toward the door.

Jase looks back at me when I don't join them. "Are you coming?"

"I'm going to wait here, see if they come back."

Hugh's expression is sympathetic, but I can't read anything else on the faces of the guys I've known my entire adult life, before they turn and walk out.

MAX AND AVA don't return, so I end up calling Dave to come get me and take me back to the hotel. I get to my room to see Ava standing outside of it. She's kicked off her shoes, is leaning against the wall by the door, arms folded. She doesn't move until I get close, then she pushes away to touch my swollen mouth.

"I'm so sorry," she murmurs.

I take her hand and kiss it so she knows it's no big deal, then reach past her to open the door.

"Are you okay?" I ask, taking her in my arms once the door is closed behind us, needing to just feel her against me. Just feel her arms around me, her breath against my throat.

"I'm okay. I'm sorry it happened that way."

"Me too. You and Max...?"

"We'll be okay. I'm more worried about *you* and Max. He wanted to wait for you tonight, but maybe it's better if you both sleep on it. Maybe meet for coffee before we head to Lisbon?"

I grumble, because it's after three now. I think we're leaving the hotel at noon. "Yeah, okay. Stay with me tonight?"

She steps back, unbuttoning her jacket, shrugs out of it to reveal a pretty camisole beneath, unzips her skirt. I get hard, of course, but tonight I just want to hold her, just want to look at her. Make sure she knows that the words I told her are the truth.

I sit on the bed to take off my boots, rise again to shuck my jeans while she watches. Then I take her hand and bring her down to the bed with me, so we're facing each other, our heads on the pillow.

I stroke her hair back from her face, touch her cheek, because I have to touch her. "I haven't told anyone I love them in a very long time."

A smile curves her lips, brightens her eyes even in the dimly lit room. "I've never told anyone."

My heart gives a kick at that. I'm not sure if it's pleasure or fear. She's young, so that could make sense, but I never thought I'd be someone's first love again. "Never?"

"I wasn't even sure that was what this was. It kind of snuck up on me." She slides her hand up between us and places her slim hand on my jaw, her fingers toying with my hair. "Scares me a little."

I give a laugh that's just relief, I think, easing the tension in my gut. "I'm scared as hell. I haven't been in a relationship in so long. I'm going to fuck up. I don't want to fuck up, but I know I will. Not—not fuck around," I clarify quickly when I see her brows lower. "I wouldn't do that." I'm positive of that, if no one else is. "But I'm going to do something wrong or say something wrong or not say something when you want me to, you know? I don't know how to be a boyfriend, but I'm going to do my best. And you—you don't be afraid to tell me what you want, what will make you happy. Because that's what I want for us." Like the other guys have, but I don't add that.

"You know I won't be afraid of that," she says, a smile curving her lips. "But I am afraid."

I cover her hand with mine, know she can feel my pulse beneath her hand. "We'll feel our way through it together, then. Focus on each other and not anyone else's expectations."

She draws in a breath, and I think she's going to say something, but then she nods. "I think that's the perfect solution to all this. You and me first, everyone else after. I think it's the only way to make it work."

I kiss her softly, gently, then she tucks her head under my chin and sighs. I wrap my arms around her and listen to her breathing soften into sleep.

Yeah. This is the real deal.

THE FOLLOWING MORNING MY PHONE—WHICH I have forgotten to put on the charger—rings at an ungodly hour. I release Ava—we were both so tired we hadn't even pulled down the bedding, just fell asleep on top of the bed—and scramble to get it while she moans awake behind me.

Max. Fuck. I have to deal with that. I'd felt so peaceful when I'd gone to sleep last night.

"Yeah?"

"Hotel restaurant. Now." And hangs up.

When he does, I see a multitude of text bubbles on my screen. I plug in the phone and turn to see Ava sitting in the middle of the bed.

"Well, I guess it's good he doesn't want to meet me in the alley or something," I say, trying to joke it off. I'd like to shower first, but really don't want to put this off any longer. "You going to be okay?"

"Are you?"

I push both hands through my hair. Man, I want a shower.

"Yeah, fine. We've been friends for a long time. It'll be fine." I lean onto the bed and kiss her. "I'll see you on the bus."

I gird myself as I take the elevator down. I'm surprised to see Max pacing in front of the entrance to the restaurant. He glowers at me, glances at my clothes—the ones I wore on stage last night, and his expression darkens.

"Did you spend the night with my daughter last night?"

Maybe I overestimated the fact that he wouldn't punch me in public again, because he looks like he wants to.

"You want to go in and get some coffee?" I ask instead of answering, motioning behind him. Maybe he's already had too much coffee, which is why he's pacing. Then I wonder at the wisdom of offering him a hot beverage he can use as a weapon.

He sets his jaw and leads the way into the crowded restaurant. Clearly he's already made arrangements for a booth for us. I'm suddenly starving, but wonder if I'll be able to swallow anything, the way he's looking at me. But I place an order anyway while he seethes.

I motion with my fingers, like I'm in *The Matrix* or something. "Let me have it."

"Of all the women you could have chosen to sleep with, you pick my daughter?" His voice gets loud, then softens as he realizes people are looking. "And don't tell me you didn't know it was wrong, or you wouldn't have been hiding it from me."

I don't hide my flinch. Instead I raise my chin. "If I'd come to you and asked you, what would you have said?"

He doesn't miss a beat. "Abso-fucking-lutely not."

I lift a hand in concession. "And so we tested things out to see how it would go before we let anyone know."

"No. You shouldn't have looked at her, shouldn't have touched her, out of respect for our friendship. All you had to do was stay away from her."

"I didn't want to stay away from her. I like her. She's smart and fresh and savvy. We have fun together." I think about that first night in London, how much joy she had, how I'd needed to absorb that to counter my own cynicism.

"She's ten years younger than you."

I nod. "That's a consideration, I know. She...might not really know what she wants yet. I'm willing to take a chance that when this tour is over, she might not want me. But I can tell you, I haven't felt this way about a woman in a long time."

He winces when I use the word *woman*.

"You never let yourself," he counters.

"That could be," I say, grateful when the waitress delivers our coffee, just to give myself something else to focus on. "Not sure why I let myself with Ava, except that she's different."

"Different how?"

I shrug one shoulder. "I just—like everything about her. I like spending time with her, I like looking over from the stage and seeing her. Just...everything is better when she's around."

His glower softens—marginally—to skeptical. "Maybe it's because you were keeping a secret, and that was different for you."

I'd wondered that too. It had definitely added to our excitement, but once we were behind closed doors, the only thing that excited me was her.

I cannot say that to her father, though.

"Maybe, but I don't think so. I mean, most of the band caught on, so it was really just you who didn't know."

His face reddens at that, and I wonder for the first time *why* he hadn't caught on. We were only sort of discreet, apparently.

"She made it clear that I don't have the right to tell her what to do, and I get that." Now he's looking at his hands on the table. "But you knew. You knew your involvement with her would bother me, and you did it anyway."

"I knew," I admit. "I didn't want to make you mad, but she just...she's something special, Max."

He looks up at me then, and I've known the guy for over ten years, but I cannot read his expression. Then he leans forward, his expression fierce.

"I'm going to be watching every move you make with her. If you make one mistake, if she sheds one tear—"

I hold out a hand to stop him. "That's fucking ridiculous. You wouldn't have had that expectation of any other boyfriend." Whoa, did I just call myself her boyfriend? "We already talked about how this is new for both of us. We're both going to make mistakes. It's unreasonable to think we won't. But I promised her—and I'll tell you since you're so fucking worried about her—that I will do what I can to make her happy, until she can't be happy with me anymore. I'm not going to use her and toss her aside. She deserves more."

"She deserves more than both of us," he mutters.

Frustration takes over. Nothing I say is going to reassure him, and I'm tired of trying. He's right, she deserves better than both of us, but I'm going to work to be worthy of her. "Look, the effort I will make with Ava is because of Ava. It's not because you're my friend, or you threaten to kick my ass, all right? It will be one hundred percent because of her. Do you understand?" I'd started to ask if he was satisfied with that but I realize I don't owe him that. I owe him a lot—he's helped us become the band we are, and he's been a good friend. But I only want two people in this relationship, and the most important one is Ava.

Even though I'm starving and I've barely had any of the coffee, I slide out of the booth, ready to get back to her. Max gives me another one of those unreadable looks as I stand by the table, then he nods, and I turn to go find Ava.

. . .

She's not in the room when I get there. I get it. She has to go pack her stuff. But I thought she would be more eager to hear what went on with me and her dad. I'll have to wait and tell her tonight.

I shower quickly, get my stuff together, check my phone—which is only about twenty percent charged. The clock shows me that it's past time to get on the bus. I'm still hungry, but there will be snacks on the plane.

I'm not the last one on the bus, though. I get my stuff stowed and look around for Ava, but she's not here. My heart does a weird lurch. Where is she?

Max is here, but he's not looking at me.

I don't find two seats together, where I can sit with Ava when she shows up, but Callan scoots over on one of the long benches to make space for me.

And then Ava steps on the bus. She looks—different. Her hair is loose and shiny around her shoulders, she's wearing her usual suit jacket, but over an Obscure Magic t-shirt and jeans, and she's still wearing those heels she loves. I always love seeing her, but seeing her like this, more relaxed and casual, makes me happy, and my smile spreads as I lean forward.

Callan grunts and stands up, offering her his seat. I flash him a look of gratitude, which he ignores, and I turn back to Ava.

She stows her bag under the seat, then sits beside me and links her fingers through mine. Okay. We are all out in the open now.

I pull out my phone and go to my contacts, tap on "Monica" as the bus pulls away from the curb.

"You're changing it?" she asks, leaning against my arm.

I look at her, bemused. "Everyone knows now. No more need for code words."

"I kind of like it," she says. "I mean, I love that we both had the same idea. That, to me, was what pushed me over the edge into love."

I hesitate, change her info back to "Monica," and save. When I look back at her, she's beaming at me, like just that little thing pleased her. And that—knowing I made her happy only makes me want to do it again and again and again.

She settles against me for the ride to the airport, content and relaxed.

And everything in me is complete.

EPILOGUE

Ava

I STEP out onto the rooftop restaurant in Paris, one year to the day that we arrived for the tour. We even have the same room downstairs, looking out on the Eiffel Tower. The room where Sawyer had left me to get ready for dinner.

I look around for him, and get a little kick of surprise when he stands up, dressed in a suit that fits like a glove. He tugs at the jacket, not entirely comfortable.

I didn't even know he had a suit. And when had he changed? I'm frozen in place for a minute before the hostess urges me forward.

Because I'm so focused on him—why wouldn't I be, because damn, he cleans up nice—I don't notice the table set up with champagne and two glasses until I'm almost standing at it. My heart starts thundering when he goes down on one knee.

I have seen girls slap a hand to their chest in surprise, and I always thought it was cliche, but honestly, it's the only reaction I have.

"Sawyer," I manage.

"Ava." He takes my hand. "My life hasn't been the same since you came into it. I thought I was happy before, but it was nothing—nothing—like how happy I am with you. Life is just —different. Better in a way I thought it would never be."

He holds up the box and flicks it open to reveal a square-cut diamond, surrounded by smaller stones. He angles it to catch the light, and I'm dazzled, but not just by the ring. I only give it a glance and look into his blue eyes. His brows dip momentarily, and he glances toward the ring.

"We can change it, if you don't like it. But I've never felt this way about anyone before, Ava. Every time I see you, I feel this joy, this...I don't know, it's like a puzzle piece clicking into place. Like I'm complete. I want that for the rest of my life. Will you say yes?"

I'm twenty-three. I never thought I'd get married so young.

I never thought I'd marry a rock star.

I never thought I'd get a proposal from that rock star on a rooftop in Paris.

I never thought I'd drop down to my knees in front of him, take his face—his handsome, beloved face—in my hands, as I say, "I will. Yes."

Sawyer

I'm the lead guitar player for the biggest band in the United States, and I am enjoying every minute of it. The fame, the money, the ladies, the untamed lifestyle.

Enter Ava, our manager's daughter, a beautiful smart young

woman who becomes our tour's media coordinator. Alongside her comes a documentary crew, ready to capture every unguarded moment. I know our worlds should never collide, yet I can't stay away. I know it's a risk. Her dad, my longtime friend, will kill me if I get involved with her.

Ava

ARMED with a freshly minted communications degree and a determination to make my mark, I step into the chaotic realm of the music industry. Drawn by my father's invitation and my own ambition, I find myself on tour with the band that has always overshadowed my relationship with him. Little do I know that this journey will be more than a chance to prove myself – it will ignite a spark I never saw coming.

Thrown into close quarters with the enigmatic Sawyer, I discover that behind the rockstar persona lies a man who challenges my perceptions. The warnings about his reputation fade as we give into our attraction. But when a documentary crew captures every unguarded glance and lingering touch, the struggle to keep our secret becomes a thrilling game of risk.

ABOUT THE AUTHOR

Emma Jay has been writing longer than she'd care to admit, using her endless string of celebrity crushes as inspiration for her heroes. Emma, married 35 years (wed at the age of 8, of course) believes writing romance is like falling in love, over and over again. Creating characters and love stories is an addiction she has no intention of breaking.

Also by Emma Jay

HISTORICALS

Eye of the Beholder

Wild Wild Widow

In the Marshal's Arms

Stealing the Marshal's Heart

CONTEMPORARIES

It Happened One Night series

One Crazy Night

One Rockin' Night

One Steamy Night

One Sizzling Night

One Wanton Night

One Smokin' Night

Taming the Cowboy series

At the Cowboy's Mercy

The Cowboy's Saving Grace

Faith in the Cowboy

Bridesmaids in Paradise series

Her Perfect Getaway

Her Island Fantasy

Her Moonlit Gamble

Blackwolf Hot Shot series

All on the Line

Crossing the Line

Standing on the Line

Standalones

Riding Out the Storm

Two Step Temptation

Show Off

Off Limits

Lessons for Teacher

Two Nights on the Island

Hot and Bothered

Milton Keynes UK
Ingram Content Group UK Ltd.
UKHW010935280823
427620UK00001B/67